Gargoylz

Wild in the Woods

Gargoylz: grotesque stone creatures found on old buildings, spouting rainwater from the guttering. Sometimes seen causing mischief and mayhem before scampering away over rooftops.

Sticky Toy Instructions

1) Remove your gargoyle sticky toy from the packaging.
2) Throw the toy firmly against a window or other smooth surface.
3) Watch your gargoyle scramble down the window, pulling funny faces.

Note:

Do not throw the toy at anyone's face
Do not throw the toy near fire
Harmless, but do not eat
May stain absorbent surfaces

Made in China  CE

D0673384

Read all the Gargoylz adventures!

Gargoylz on the Loose!

Gargoylz Get Up to Mischief

Gargoylz at a Midnight Feast

Gargoylz Take a Trip

Gargoylz Put on a Show

Gargoylz Have Fun at the Fair

Gargoylz Go to a Party

Gargoylz: Magic at the Museum

Gargoylz Make a Splash!

Gargoylz Ride to the Rescue

Gargoylz Make a Movie

Gargoylz Summer Fun

Gargoylz on the Go!

Gargoylz Save Christmas

Gargoylz: Mess at the Mill

Also available:

Gargoylz Make Some Noise

Gargoylz

Wild in the Woods

Burchett & Vogler

illustrated by Leighton Noyes

RED FOX

GARGOYLZ: WILD IN THE WOODS

A RED FOX BOOK 978 1 849 41463 0

Published in Great Britain by Red Fox Books,
an imprint of Random House Children's Books
A Random House Company

This edition published 2011

1 3 5 7 9 10 8 6 4 2

Series created and developed by Amber Caravéo
Copyright © Random House Children's Books, 2011 All rights reserved.

The Random House Group Limited supports the Forest Stewardship Council®
(FSC®), the leading international forest certification organisation. All our titles
that are printed on Greenpeace approved FSC® certified paper carry the FSC®
logo. Our paper procurement policy can be found at
www.randomhouse.co.uk/environment

MIX
Paper from
responsible sources
FSC® C016897

Set in 15/20pt Bembo Schoolbook by Falcon Oast Graphic Art Ltd

Red Fox Books are published by Random House Children's Books,
61–63 Uxbridge Road, London W5 5SA

www.**kids**at**randomhouse**.co.uk
www.**totallyrandombooks**.co.uk
www.**randomhouse**.co.uk

Addresses for companies within The Random House Group Limited can be
found at: www.randomhouse.co.uk/offices.htm

THE RANDOM HOUSE GROUP Limited Reg. No. 954009

A CIP catalogue record for this book is available from the British Library

Printed and bound in Great Britain by CPI Bookmarque, Croydon, CR0 4TD

For Heather, Oliver and Elliott Chang, and in memory
of Mo and his legendary camping curries
- **Burchett & Vogler**

For Ellison who isn't afraid of monsters because
monsters are afraid of him!
- **Leighton Noyes**

Gargoylz Fact File

Full name: Tobias the Third
Known as: Toby
Special Power: Flying
Likes: All kinds of pranks and mischief - especially playing jokes on the vicar
Dislikes: Mrs Hogsbottom, garden gnomes

Full name: Barnabas
Known as: Barney
Special Power: Making big stinks!
Likes: Cookiez
Dislikes: Being surprised by humanz

Name: Eli
Special Power: Turning into a grass snake
Likes: Sssports Day, Sssslithering

Full name: Enoch
Special Power: Doing the voices of any character he's ever read about
Likes: Exciting stories and learning new pranks
Dislikes: Loud, scary noises

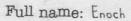

Full name: Bartholomew

Known as: Bart

Special Power: Burping spiders

Likes: Being grumpy

Dislikes: Being told to cheer up

Full name: Theophilus

Known as: Theo

Special Power: Turning into a ferocious tiger (well, tabby kitten!)

Likes: Sunny spots and cosy places

Dislikes: Rain

Full name: Zackary

Known as: Zack

Special Power: Making himself invisible to humanz

Likes: Bouncing around, eating bramblz, thistlz, and anything with pricklz!

Dislikes: Keeping still

Full name: Jehieli
Known as: Jelly
Special Power: Turning to jelly
Likes: Having friendz to play with
Dislikes: Bulliez and spoilsports

Name: Ira
Special Power: Making it rain
Likes: Making humanz walk the plank
Dislikes: Being bored

Name: Cyrus
Special Power: Singing lullabies to send humanz to sleep
Likes: Fun dayz out
Dislikes: Snoring

Name: Rufus
Special Power: Turning into a skeleton
Likes: Playing spooky tricks
Dislikes: Squeezing into small spaces

Full name: Nebuchadnezzar
Known as: Neb
Special Power: Changing colour to match his background
Likes: Snorkelling
Dislikes: Anyone treading on his tail

Name: Azzan
Special Power: Breathing fire
Likes: Surprises
Dislikes: Smoke going up his nose and making him sneeze

Full name: Abel
Special Power: Turning into a tree
Likes: Funny puns and word jokes
Dislikes: Dogs weeing up against him

Name: Ruben
Special Power: Can go anywhere in the world in a blink of an eye
Likes: Mrs Santa's baking
Dislikes: Delivering Christmas presents to houses where there aren't any snackz for Santa and his reindeer

School Report - Max Black

Days absent: 2

Days late: 5

Max is a bright boy. If he spent as much time on his school work as he does on annoying Lucinda Tellingly he would get much better marks. I am pleased to see that he enjoys exercise - although I do not count running down corridors making racing car noises. Also I would be glad if he did not shout "Awesome" quite so loudly every time we have football practice.

Class teacher - Miss Deirdre Bleet

The only good thing I can say about Max Black is that he is always early for school. However, he is the last one into the classroom. He spends far too much time playing tricks with Ben Neal. Mrs Pumpkin is still off sick after discovering an earwig farm in her handbag. Max ignores all school rules. He has recently developed a curious interest in drainpipes and has been seen talking to the wall. This behaviour is outrageous and must stop.

Head teacher - Hagatha Hogsbottom (Mrs)

School Report - Ben Neal

Days absent: 1

Days late: 6

Ben has many abilities which he does not always use. He works very hard at dreaming up tricks to play, which gives him very little time to concentrate on his learning. He enjoys football and skateboarding - indeed, he and his board can frequently be found upside down in a flowerbed.

Class teacher - Miss Deirdre Bleet

Ben Neal is a strange boy. He is often to be found grinning at gutters.

He constantly breaks school rule number 742: boys must not break school rules.

Ben thinks he can get away with anything by flashing his blue eyes and looking innocent. I am not fooled. Indeed I am still waiting for him and Max Black to write a note of apology to Mr Bucket the caretaker. Gluing his wellington boots to the staffroom ceiling was outrageous!

Head teacher - Hagatha Hogsbottom (Mrs)

Contents

1. The Terrible Team Mix-Up   1

2. Tent Disaster   27

3. Treasure Hunt Tricks   57

4. The Monster of Ferny Forest   81

1. The Terrible Team Mix-Up

Br . . . ring! Not a moment too soon, the
bell sounded for playtime. Max Black was
up from his desk and at the classroom door
in four seconds flat.

"Four seconds is a new superspy record,"
he told his best friend, Ben Neal, who was
skidding to a halt beside him. "Time for
some fun."

"Superspies like us deserve fun," said
Ben. "We've just survived thirty minutes of
long division!"

1

"Max Black and Ben Neal, where are you going?"

The boys spun round. Their weedy teacher was peering at them over her half-moon glasses. She looked like a puzzled gerbil.

"Off to the playground, miss," said Max.  He went to follow the rest of the class filing out.

"Didn't you hear me read out your names?" quavered Miss Bleet. She flapped a piece of paper at them. "You've got to stay in."

Max and Ben looked at each other in horror. This sounded like bad news.

"We must be in trouble," muttered Ben.

"But how?" Max hissed back. "No one

could know it was us who put up that sign saying *School Closed Due to Outbreak of Martian Mumps* on the gate."

"One of our best tricks ever." Ben chuckled behind his hand.

"It's about the weekend," said Miss Bleet. "Your mums have signed you up for—"

Before she could finish, the door burst open and the boys were knocked flying.

"Get out of my way," came a gruff voice.

Max switched on his spy radar. Shaved head, big fists, eyebrows like fierce beetles. He knew what that meant. It was Enemy Agent Barry Price, also known as The Basher, codename: School Bully. Barry stomped over and took a seat in the front row, followed by more children from Year Four.

Max nudged Ben. "Whatever we're in for, it's going to be a lot worse now Barry's here."

"And I've just spotted Lucinda Tellingly and her friends," groaned Ben. "I'd rather give up football for a week than have anything to do with those gruesome girls."

"Listen, everyone," Miss Bleet called feebly as some more children from Barry's class ran in and took their places. "Are you all ready to talk about our exciting camping trip this weekend?"

The other children nodded, but Max and Ben looked at each other in delight. They'd never been on a school camping holiday before!

"Awesome!" cried Max.

"But of course,

this is only for children who don't play tricks, Max and Ben," Miss Bleet went on.

The boys gulped. Had she found out about the notice on the gate after all?

"Miss Drew has not forgotten the time you flooded her art class," their teacher continued.

"That wasn't a trick," explained Ben in relief. "It was educational. We were trying to sink our *Titanic* model."

"Perhaps, but what about the day you used Mrs Simmer's special custard ladle as a catapult?"

"We only borrowed it for a science experiment," insisted Max. "It was the right shape for launching our mud missiles."

"That may be," said their teacher, "but we were picking grass out of our trifle for days. Any more of that behaviour and you won't be coming."

"We'll be good," chorused the boys eagerly.

"I hope so," said Miss Bleet doubtfully. "Now, down to business. Our head teacher always comes on school camping trips . . ."

"Disaster," whispered Ben. "Mrs Hogsbum will ruin it."

"She'll make up new, super strict camping rules especially for us!" Max gasped.

". . . but this year Mrs Hogsbottom is going bungee jumping and can't make it," finished Miss Bleet.

"That's awesome!" shouted Max. "I mean . . . that's awful."

"So we need some parents to come along and help out," Miss Bleet told them. "Max's dad has already volunteered."

"I might have known," groaned Max. "He's always going on about how he was in the Cubs and how he used to put up the tents and—"

"*My* dad will be much more use," Barry butted in rudely. "We go camping together all the time."

"I've got a bad feeling about this," Ben muttered to Max. "Imagine – two Bashers together!"

"That would be excellent. I'll telephone your father and ask him, Barry," said Miss Bleet. "Now, just to make the trip extra fun, I've divided you into two teams and there are going to be some exciting challenges over the weekend."

She stuck a piece of paper onto the board. It had two lists of names on it. "Check which team you're in, then run along for the rest of playtime." She sat down and began to mark their maths books. "When the bell goes I'll see you in the hall. You're going to practise working together, ready for the weekend, while the rest of the year has nature studies in the field."

Barry stood up. "I don't need to check which team I'm in," he announced. "It'll be the best anyway, because I'll be in it."

And he swaggered out.

Lucinda, Poppy and Tiffany rushed up to the lists.

"We're in the Mice team, girls," cried Lucinda in delight.

"That's a lovely name," sighed Poppy and Tiffany. They held hands and skipped out to play.

Max and Ben went up to the board.

"Let's see what team she's put us in," said Max.

"Mice and Rabbits!" said Ben in disgust, reading the paper.

"What stupid names."

"Oh no," groaned Max. "I'm a Mouse – with the gruesome girls. Although Duncan and Gavin are in that team too, so it's not so bad. But where's your name?"

"I'm in the Rabbits," croaked Ben, going pale. "And I'm with The Basher!"

"That's not right!" cried Max, reading the list again.

"We're always together," agreed Ben.

"We've got to change this," declared Max. "And we're going to need help."

"Time to find the gargoylz!" said Ben.

"Race you to the playground!"

The gargoylz were Max and Ben's secret friends. The ugly little stone creatures lived on the church next door to Oldacre Primary School and always came to the rescue when the boys needed them. Nobody else in the world knew that the gargoylz could come to life.

"There they are!" yelled Max. The boys raced up to the wall that looked over the churchyard. "I can see Toby and Theo and

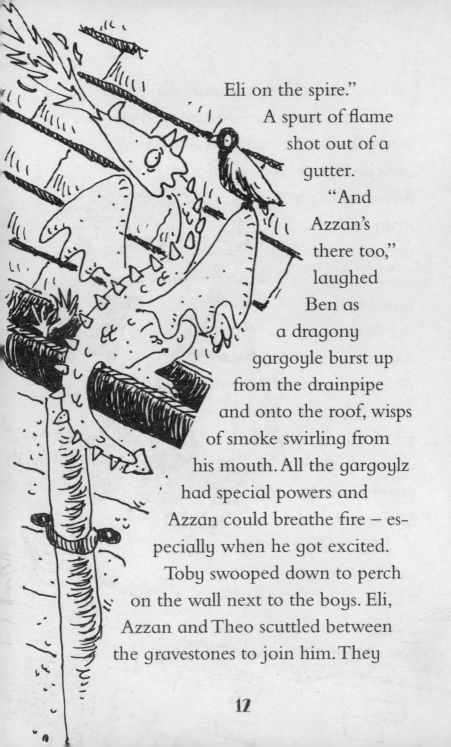

Eli on the spire."
A spurt of flame
shot out of a
gutter.
"And
Azzan's
there too,"
laughed
Ben as
a dragony
gargoyle burst up
from the drainpipe
and onto the roof, wisps
of smoke swirling from
his mouth. All the gargoylz
had special powers and
Azzan could breathe fire – especially when he got excited.
Toby swooped down to perch
on the wall next to the boys. Eli,
Azzan and Theo scuttled between
the gravestones to join him. They

quickly scanned the area to make sure that
there were no other humans around.

"Greetingz!" said Toby. A look of
mischief came over his monkey face.
"Have you got time to play some trickz
with us?"

"Not now," said Ben.

"But we always play trickz with you!"
said Azzan. "Are you ill?"

"It's worse than that," said Max. "We've
got a humungous problem."

"And we need your help," explained
Ben.

The long knobbly branch of a nearby
tree poked him in the back. "What do you
want us to do?" asked the tree as it slowly
turned into a twiggy-looking gargoyle.

"Hello, Abel," said Max.

"Listen, gargoylz. There's been a Terrible Team Mix-Up!"

He told them all about the camping trip and Miss Bleet's lists. The gargoylz shuddered when they heard the wimpy team names.

"Camping sssoundz fun though," hissed Eli, and the snakes on his head nodded in agreement. "Can we come?"

"Of course you can," said Ben. "That would make the weekend absolutely amazing. But first we need you to help us think of a way to get my name off the Rabbits and onto the Mice list."

"We can't do it ourselves because Miss Bleet's in there," said Max.

"I can change into a tree and hook the list out of the window," suggested Abel.

"Our teacher may be a bit dopey," said Ben, "but I think she'd notice a branch waving about all over the classroom."

"I could turn into a grasss sssnake and ssslither off with the lissst," said Eli. His snakes chuckled merrily.

"That would be great," said Max. "But there's one problem. Snakes can't climb classroom walls."

Theo stretched and showed his claws. "I'll use my special power and scare Miss Bleet into changing the list."

"I'm not sure . . ." began Ben doubtfully.
Theo thought he could turn into a fierce
tiger, but as he was a very young gargoyle
– only four hundred and twelve – he
hadn't quite got his special power right
yet, and always turned into a sweet kitten.
Nobody liked to tell him, though, in case
his feelings were hurt.

"That's a very good plan, Theo,"
declared Toby. He winked at Max
and Ben. "Don't worry, boyz. Leave it
with us."

The gargoylz got into a huddle to make
their plan. Then Theo changed into a
kitten, jumped down and scampered over

to the classroom door, which was slightly ajar. He slipped inside and was gone. Toby flew up to the open classroom window.

"I'm not missing this, Agent Neal," said Max.

"Too right, Agent Black," agreed Ben. "Let's spy on the action. We'll use our superspeedy sneaking machines — codename: feet."

They raced along to join Toby and they all peered in.

Max gave a gasp. "Theo's coming through the door. He's turned into a kitten."

"He'll never scare Miss Bleet like that!" groaned Ben. "This plan isn't going to work."

Theo gave a loud miaow and started rubbing round their teacher's legs.

"What a dear little cat!" exclaimed Miss Bleet in a gooey voice. "But you can't stay here."

With that she scooped Theo up and carried him out into the corridor.

As soon as she'd gone, Toby swooped in over the boys' heads, snatched a pencil and rubber from Miss Bleet's desk and flew over to the list.

"The plan's working after all!" whispered Max. "Theo's got rid of Miss Bleet."

"But not in the way he thought," chuckled Ben.

Toby flew back out of the window and perched on Ben's shoulder. "Congratulationz," he told him. "You're both in the Wolves team."

"But there isn't a Wolves team," said Max, puzzled.

Toby grinned. "There is now! You said Mice was a stupid name so I changed it to Wolves."

"Cool!" gasped Ben. "Thanks, Toby."

Miss Bleet appeared in the playground carrying Theo. She put the little kitten down and fondly watched him scamper off to the church wall. Max and Ben shot away from the window and whistled an innocent tune until she'd gone back inside.

Then they dashed over to join their friends.

"Did you see the fear on Miss Bleet's face?" asked Theo eagerly, back in his gargoyle shape. "I scared her good and proper."

"Dangling drainpipes!" said Toby. "I haven't had so much fun since we added fifteen packets of cookiez to the vicar's shopping list and had a scrumptious feast when he wasn't looking."

The bell clanged loudly for the end of playtime.

"See you later, gargoylz," called Max as he and Ben shot into the hall to join the other campers.

"OK, everyone," warbled Miss Bleet, peering short-sightedly at her lists. "Get into your groups. Wolves on the

left . . . that's strange, I could have sworn
that team was called the Mice."

"It is," said Lucinda.

"I seem to have
written *Wolves* by
mistake," said
their teacher in
surprise, sticking the
list on the wall bars.

"We don't want
to be Wolves,"
sulked Poppy.

"Mice is such a
nice, fluffy name,"
added Tiffany.

"Indeed . . ."
began Miss Bleet.

"Miss Bleet, you can't change it now,"
called Max. "It wouldn't be fair."

"That's right," agreed Ben. "It would
be really mean of you to make our poor
teacher do all that extra writing, girls."

Lucinda and her friends scowled and stomped across to join Max, Ben and the rest of the Wolves. Lucinda frowned when she saw that Ben was standing with them.

"Miss!" she piped up in an annoying whine. "Miss! Ben's not meant to be in this team."

"Yes I am," said Ben. "My name's on the list." He gave her one of his special innocent looks. It always worked on the dinner ladies, who gave him extra fish fingers. It didn't work on Lucinda.

"It can't be," she insisted, flouncing over to Miss Bleet's piece of paper. "I should know. I read the list twice. Listen. The Wolves are – Max, Duncan, Gavin, Lucinda, Poppy, Tiffany, Ben ..." She gawped at the list.

"You read out Ben's

name, Lucinda," called
Poppy helpfully.

"Just after mine,"
added Tiffany.

"I know," snapped
Lucinda, going red.
"But it wasn't there
before."

"Girls," quavered Miss
Bleet. "This sort of thing won't
help you bond as a happy group. You've
got to work together . . . although I'm sure
I put Max and Ben in separate teams."

"They must have changed the list!"
snarled Lucinda, pointing an accusing
finger at the boys.

"We never touched it," said Max. "Cross
my heart and may my pants fall down if
I'm lying."

"Your pants are safe," whispered Ben.
"After all, it wasn't us who changed the
list, it was Toby!"

"I saw the boys out in the playground, Lucinda," said Miss Bleet, "so they can't have done it. Get back to your group and we'll have some happy bonding." She clapped her hands for attention. "Now, Wolves and Rabbits, hold hands with your teammates and make a friendship circle."

"Rabbits?" bellowed Barry. "I didn't know our team was called the Rabbits!"

"I chose nice woodland names for nice woodland campers like us," Miss Bleet tried to explain.

"But Wolves isn't a nice woodland name," Lucinda persisted.

"Wolves live in woods," put in Ben.

"Rabbits is a stupid name," said Barry. "I'm going to be a Wolf!"

He set off towards the opposite team, who began to quake.

"Why don't you call yourselves the Bears?" suggested Max quickly.

"Yes," said Ben. "They're bigger

than Wolves – and fiercer."

Barry turned back to his team. "Right, Rabbits, we're the Bears from now on."

The other Bears gulped and nodded.

"Glad that's sorted," squeaked Miss Bleet, wiping her forehead. "Now into your friendship circles."

"Ha ha!" burst out Barry. "Look at Max and Ben holding hands with girls! Their team should be called the Wimps, not the Wolves."

"I'm glad the gargoylz are coming camping too, Agent Black," Ben whispered to Max when the ordeal of the friendship circle was over. "It looks like we might need some help with Barry."

"You're right, Agent Neal," Max whispered back. "I'm sure they'd be delighted to play some tricks if he bashes about too much."

"Miss!" Lucinda complained. "Max and Ben are whispering when they should be bonding."

Ben turned and beamed at their teacher. "I was just saying that this weekend's going to be super cool!"

Five stony faces suddenly popped up at the hall window and waved merrily at the boys.

"I agree!" exclaimed Max. "We're *all* going to have an awesome time!"

2. Tent Disaster

Max and Ben sat at the back of the coach.
Friday afternoon had raced round and
they were now whizzing along to the
campsite for their exciting weekend. They
were clutching their bulging rucksacks
tightly on their laps.

"Keep still, Azzan!" hissed Max as his
bag wriggled. "Someone will see."

"Sorry!" There was a growly chuckle
from inside the bag and a wisp of smoke
curled out. "My tail got stuck up Toby's nose."

Abel's knobbly stone fingers poked out
Ben's rucksack and prodded him in the

tummy. "Eli wants to know if we're there yet."

"Hope ssso," called Eli. "I'm fed up with Ira sssinging pirate sssongz in my ear."

"Yo ho ho and a bottle of milk!" chirped Ira, sticking his beak out. The parroty gargoyle had taken Theo's place on the trip. Theo had decided that camping sounded too uncomfortable and he'd stayed at home, curled up on the vicar's chimney.

"What's that you're singing?" called Max's dad from the front of the coach.

"Just a little song to make the journey go quicker!" Ben answered quickly, clamping Ira's beak shut.

"Good idea," said Mr Black. "When I was a Cub we always sang on journeys.

Come on, everyone." He began to
belt out a song at the top of his voice,
making Miss Bleet jump. "Row, row,
row your boat . . . "

Max slumped down in
embarrassment as
some of the children
began to titter. "At
least Barry's not
here to scoff," he
murmured. "It was a
great result when he
said his dad would
be bringing him
separately."

"I wish he wasn't
coming at all," said
Ben. "We've got
to make sure he
doesn't spoil this weekend."

"Leave it to usss," hissed Eli.

"You mean *leaf* it to us," chuckled Abel.

"Did you like my joke, boyz? I said *leaf* instead of *leave*. That was a pun — because I'm a tree, you see, with leaves ..."

The rucksacks began to shake with laughter.

"I love that joke," called Toby. "Even if you've told it a hundred times. It's still funny."

"And punny," added Abel, making the rucksacks chortle even more loudly.

The coach swung through a gate and along a bumpy road.

"Welcome to Ferny Forest," announced Miss Bleet. "Rabbits and Mice ... I mean Wolves and Bears ... your camping adventure starts now!"

Max and Ben heaved their rucksacks on and struggled off the coach. The road had taken them deep into the woods and gnarly, twisted branches hung over their heads.

"Awesome, Agent Neal!" exclaimed Max, gazing at the trees. "Ferny Forest looks really wild and mysterious!"

"We're going to have a great weekend, Agent Black," grinned Ben. "And so will the gargoylz."

Miss Bleet led the way along a path from the car park to a clearing in the dense woods. The boys plonked their bags down near a thick leafy bush at the

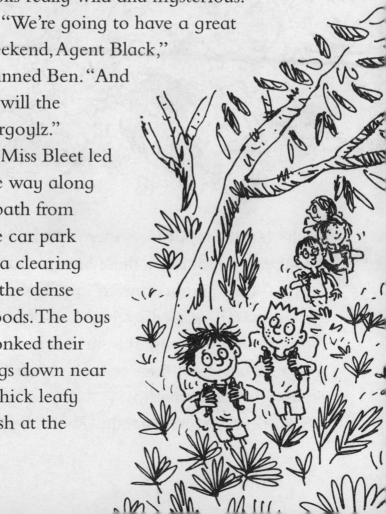

edge of the clearing and undid the flaps.

Ira hopped out of Ben's rucksack and rearranged his stony feathers. "Look lively, me hearties!" he squawked. "This may not

be the high seas but I bet there's pirate treasure to be found in these here woodz."

The others jumped out to join him.

"Treasure?" gasped Azzan. "Let's start hunting straight away. If I burn down a few treez we won't have to look so hard." He took a deep breath.

"No!" said Max urgently. "We'd all

have to go home if there was a forest fire!"

"I'll make sure he doesn't," promised Toby. "Come on, gargoylz. Let's have a snack first. This place is full of delicious bramblz and thistlz and lots of thingz with pricklz."

"Hold your tongue, you scurvy knave!" squawked Ira. "I'm the captain of this crew. I say when we have a snack." He pointed a wing at a spiky blackberry bush. "Snack time!"

A loud *honk* echoed around the forest. The gargoylz scrambled out of sight as a huge, shiny motor home came roaring over the rough ground. It screeched to a halt right in front of Miss Bleet.

Barry was hanging out of one window, chewing bubble gum. The driver was hanging out of the other window, chewing gum as well. Max's radar burst into life. Shaved head like The Basher's, big fists like The Basher's, nasty grin like The Basher's. He knew what that meant. It was Barry's father. Also known as Mr Price. Codename: Big Basher.

They jumped down from the cab. The Basher blew a big bubble of gum. Big Basher blew an even bigger bubble. *Pop!* It burst all over Miss Bleet's glasses.

"We'll show them what camping's all about, won't we, Dad?" yelled Barry.

"We sure

will, son," boomed Mr Price. "We're experts, we are!"

Miss Bleet wiped the gum off her glasses and clapped her hands for silence.

"Welcome, everybody," she said feebly. "I hope you're all ready for a weekend of challenges. It'll be Mice ... er ... Wolves

versus Bears, and the first challenge starts now. Mr Black, if you could go with the Wolves and Mr Price with the Bears."

Miss Bleet pointed to a pile of sacks and poles.

"Those are your tents," she told them.
"They're the old-fashioned sort. You
have to put the frame up first, the canvas
over the top, then hammer the pegs into
the ground and hook the ropes round
them . . ."

"We called them guy ropes when I was
in the Cubs," piped up Max's dad.

"I never bothered with the Cubs," said
Big Basher. "Too sissy."

"I bet they wouldn't let him join," Max
whispered to Ben.

"Now, the first challenge is to set up
your team camping areas as quickly as
you can," Miss Bleet went on. "Two to a
tent—"

"Seven for us!" came Toby's growly
voice from the bushes.

"No, Max," said Miss Bleet firmly. "The
tents are only big enough for two – or
three at most."

"I know, miss," said Max hurriedly.

"I meant . . . we'd
only take seven
minutes."

"Oh, splendid,"
said their teacher.
"The first team to
put up their tents and
light their campfire
gets a point. The
team with the most
points at the end of
the weekend will be
the winner! Now
watch me!"

She flung off
her coat. She was
wearing a shirt
covered in pockets
which bulged with
penknives, maps,
compasses and a torch. Her knobbly knees
stuck out from a pair of khaki shorts.

There was a whirl of canvas and guy ropes, and the next moment she was standing by a gleaming tent and a roaring campfire.

"See?" She beamed. "It's simple. Off you go."

The Wolves began to pick up their tent poles.

"You can give us Bears the point now," said Barry, smirking nastily. "We've already won the first challenge."

"But you haven't set up your campsite!" burst out Max.

"That's because we've brought it with us," said Barry. "My dad's motor home."

Big Basher patted him on the head. "That's right, son. I won't have my boy lying on some lumpy bit of ground in a sleeping bag."

"There's room for all the Bears," boasted Barry, "and there's an electric oven so we don't need a campfire."

"You can't do that!" gasped Ben.

"It's not fair," protested Max.

"When I was a Cub," began Mr Black, "we always—"

"THERE WILL BE NO SLEEPING IN MOTOR HOMES!" bellowed Miss Bleet.

Everyone stepped back in shock. They'd never seen their teacher look so fierce.

"This weekend is about working

together and
surviving in
the wild." She
flung out her
hand. "The keys
to your motor
home please, Mr
Price!"

Barry's dad gulped and handed them
over without a word. Miss Bleet stomped
off and began clattering some cooking
pots.

Mr Black rubbed his hands together.
"Come on, Wolves," he said cheerfully.
"Let's get busy, as we used to say in the
Cubs. I'll put my tent up over here . . ."

Half an hour later, Max and Ben had
hammered in their last tent peg. They
stood back to admire their work.

"It's a bit wonky," said Ben.

"At least we've got it up," said Max.
"Look at the girls. We'll never win the

challenge at this rate."

Lucinda, Poppy and Tiffany had managed to tie themselves up in their ropes. They were shrieking at the tops of their voices as Max's dad and Miss Bleet tried to free them.

Barry suddenly loomed over the boys.

"That's rubbish," he snarled, pointing at their tent. "I've only got to breathe on it and it'll fall down."

"At least we've got ours up," said Max bravely. "You Bears aren't doing much better."

Crash! Clumph!

Their tent collapsed in a heap as The Basher threw himself on top of it.

"Whoops," he said loudly. "I tripped!"

He ran back to his team, smashing into Duncan and Gavin's tent as he went.

"Now we've got to start again," sighed Ben. "That Barry's such a cheat."

"Need help, boyz?" asked a growly voice, and Toby's cheeky monkey face popped out from behind a bush. More stony ears and tails could be seen behind him.

"Yes please!" said Max. "It's only fair after what The Basher did."

"Gargoylz crew to the rescue, me hearties," declared Ira.

Soon the tent canvas was bulging with gargoyle shapes. In two seconds flat it was up, and Max and Ben had tightened the guy ropes.

"Thanks, you lot," whispered Max. "We'll give Duncan and Gavin a hand now."

"And I'll get some firewood," said Toby. "We'll make sure the Wolves win the challenge."

"I'm not so sure about that," replied Max. "The girls are still in a mess."

Lucinda, Poppy and Tiffany were standing helplessly around their tent, which lay in a tangled heap on the ground.

"Hopeless," groaned Ben.
When Duncan and Gavin's sleeping
quarters were up, Max
and Ben looked over to
see how the girls were
getting on. They were
now inside their floppy
tent, struggling with
the poles. Suddenly two
long branches reached
down and pulled the
roof up for them.

"Good old Abel,"
whispered Ben. "They'd
never have managed
without some twiggy help."

Now at last all the Wolves' tents were
ready. Max and Ben looked over at the
Bears. Big Basher was waving a box of
matches over a pile of wood.

"Cheating again!" muttered Ben.

"Give those to me now!" bellowed

Miss Bleet, marching over to him.

Barry's father plonked them in her hand.

"Who's on firewood duty? As we used to say in the Cubs," Mr Black asked the Wolves.

"All sorted, Dad," called Max, pointing at Toby's huge collection of sticks.

"Wow!" gasped Mr Black. "Well done, team. Let's get the fire going." He sniffed the air. "It smells like Miss Bleet is cooking something nice. The sooner we've done the challenge, the sooner we can eat."

He knelt down and chose a branch with a hole in it. He crammed the hole full of dry leaves and paper and put the end of a pointy stick into it. Then he twisted it about between his hands. "I learned this

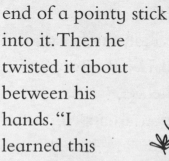

when I was a Cub," he said proudly.

A spark flashed and he blew it gently until it became a small flame. It licked around the wood and caught the dry leaves. Then he added more sticks. The Wolves cheered as their campfire leaped into life.

SPLASH . . . SIZZLE!

A shower of water fell on the fire and put it out. Behind them The Basher was holding an empty bucket.

"Whoops!" he sneered. "I tripped again."

He swaggered off to the Bears, who had finally got their tents up and were now building a pile of wood.

"Oh dear," said Mr Black, shaking his head. "That was unlucky."

"Deliberate, more like," muttered Ben under his breath.

"Quick, Dad," cried Max. "We've got to get the fire going again."

Mr Black rubbed madly at his sticks but they were too wet now.

"Time for some gargoyle help," whispered Ben.

The boys edged over to a nearby bush. "Azzan?" called Max. "We need help."

"I can see that," answered Azzan. "I'll give you a good hot blast."

"Not yet!" hissed Max. "You're too

far away.
Everyone will see what's
happening." He pointed to a
huge hollow branch on the ground.
"Hide in that," he whispered. "We'll get
you closer to the fire."

Azzan jumped into the middle of the
leaves and the boys dragged the branch
towards Max's dad.

"Well done, lads," puffed Mr Black,
bright red in the face. "I see you've got
some extra wood – but I can't get a
spark."

Ben gave Azzan a nudge with his toe. A
huge flame shot out and
the pile of twigs burst
into a crackling fire.
"Awesome, Dad!"
said Max.

Mr Black scratched his head. "It never worked as well as that when I was a Cub," he muttered.

"It's worked a bit too well!" exclaimed Ben. The branch where Azzan was hiding had begun to smoke.

The boys caught sight of a singed stony tail as the dragony gargoyle scampered off into the bushes.

"What a magnificent fire!" called Miss Bleet. "And all your tents are up too. I declare the Wolves the winners of the first challenge! One point to them."

Barry stamped his foot in fury and the Wolves cheered. All except Lucinda Tellingly. Lucinda was staring at the bushes with frightened eyes.

"What's the matter?" asked Poppy.

"I saw a monster," croaked Lucinda.

"What was it like?" asked Tiffany nervously.

"Like a dragon," said Lucinda. "I saw its tail. It was all smoky."

"There are no monsters round here, Lucinda," said Ben, hoping Azzan was well hidden. "It was probably just a twig."

"Twigs can't run," said Lucinda. "This one ran into the trees. It was a monster and it scared me!"

They all jumped as a piercing whistle blasted their eardrums.

"Time for supper!" called Miss Bleet. She was stirring a big pot over her fire. "Bring your plates up. I've prepared my special

Campers' Curried Casserole."

The two teams served themselves then sat around their fires, enjoying their food. Mr Black and Mr Price sat with Miss Bleet by her roaring fire.

"This is scrumptious!" said Ben, munching happily.

"I'm still hungry!" boomed a voice behind him. A hand reached out and snatched Ben's plate. It was The Basher.

"Bears need more food than Wolves." He gobbled down Ben's meal and looked around for more.

"That's not fair," moaned Ben as he shared Max's last few mouthfuls.

"I've had a brilliant idea, Agent Neal," whispered Max. "We can get him back for being so mean. Secret plan: Scare The Basher."

"Go for it, Agent Black," Ben whispered back.

"Lucinda saw a monster in the woods," Max said loudly.

"I'm not scared of monsters," said Barry, scraping Duncan's plate clean.

"It was the monster of Ferny Forest," said Max mysteriously.

"*You* said there weren't any monsters," quavered Lucinda.

"I know," replied Max. "That was before I remembered . . ."

"Remembered what?" breathed Tiffany.

". . . about the monster that lives deep among the trees," said Max in a hushed voice.

All the campers gathered round.

"Is that the one with hundreds of sharp teeth?" asked Ben, trying not to giggle.

"The very one," said Max, nodding solemnly.

"And claws like knives?" asked Ben.

"That's him," said Max. "He eats naughty kids for breakfast."

The Basher was staring at him, open-mouthed. "That's a load of old rubbish," he spluttered.

"Don't let the monster hear you say

that!" gasped Ben. "He gobbled up the last kid who didn't believe in him. There was nothing left of him – they only found his penknife."

Barry skulked off, looking around nervously. "It's not even a scary story," he called over his shoulder.

"Bedtime!" announced Miss Bleet. "See you all in the morning for your next challenge."

Max and Ben ran over to their tent. Max shone his torch inside and five grinning faces appeared in the beam.

"Good story, Max," said Azzan, making himself comfortable in Ben's sleeping bag.

"Spluttering gutterz!" chuckled Toby. "I haven't had so much fun since Abel turned into a horse chestnut tree and dropped conkers on the vicar's barbecue."

The boys joined their stony friends and settled down for the night.

"I'm scared, Dad," came a wail. "I want to sleep in the motor home. Ask Miss Bleet for the keys."

"You need to toughen up, son," they heard Mr Price answer. "Go to sleep."

"Our secret plan has worked," whispered Ben. "Barry won't dare be horrible any more!"

"And we can have an awesome camping trip!" added Max. "Can't we, gargoylz?"

There was no answer. The gargoylz
were already snoring their heads off!

3. Treasure Hunt Tricks

Max opened his eyes and looked around
his tent. There was no sign of the gargoylz
but something had woken him. He sniffed
the air.

"That is the most awesome smell in the
history of most awesome smells," he sighed.

Ben was already scrambling out of
his sleeping bag. "Take me to it," he
exclaimed. "It's making me so hungry."

They burst out of their tent. The Bears
sat around their campfire, tucking into
bacon and sausage sandwiches, which
oozed with gooey red ketchup.

Barry was poking sausages around a frying pan. "These are mine!" he called, waving his fork menacingly. "I'm the cook so I get the biggest."

His dad nodded. "And don't forget me, son."

"Sausages for breakfast!" gasped Max. "We'll have that too."

Lucinda Tellingly blocked his path. "No you won't. Us Wolves are eating healthily." She pressed a small bowl of dry muesli into his hand. Duncan and Gavin were already munching miserably. "Barry

pinched all the sausages for his team but we didn't want them anyway. They're not good for you."

"That's right," added Poppy, passing a bowl to Ben.

"Healthy campers win more challenges," chanted Tiffany, looking smug.

"Hungry campers can't do challenges!" groaned Ben.

"And we'll starve to death if that's all we have," muttered Max. "We've got to get our breakfast back, Agent Neal."

"You're right, Agent Black," Ben answered. "But I can't see how. The Basher's going to eat the rest of the sausages any minute . . ."

"Oi!" Barry suddenly jumped to his feet and flapped his frying pan about wildly. "Who's stolen my sausages?"

"What are you talking about, son?" asked Big Basher, appearing from his tent.

"I had six scrumptious

sausages ready to eat and now they're gone!" wailed Barry. He looked angrily across at Max and Ben.

"We haven't got them," said Max.

"And they wouldn't want them," sniffed Tiffany. "The Wolves are eating a healthy breakfast."

"Boyz!" A stony claw pulled at Max's pyjama sleeve. He turned to see Azzan poking out of a bush.

"Look what Eli's snatched for you."

The boys looked. Eli was holding three scrumptious sausages in each paw.

"Cool!"

whispered Ben. "Thanks, Eli! We'll see you in our tent."

"We've got to get dressed now," said Max loudly.

The boys bounded back into their tent to find the five gargoylz squatting on their sleeping bags.

"Do you want to share?" asked Ben, wondering how they would manage six sausages between the seven of them.

"No thanksss," said Eli, rubbing his stony tummy. "We've ssstuffed ourselves with pricklz and bramblz."

"And thistlz," added Toby. "We found a

wonderful patch under the motor home."

"Well, you saved our lives," Max told him, through a mouthful of yummy breakfast.

"I used my ssspecial power and ssslithered up to the pan when Barry was busy shouting," said Eli proudly.

"Thanks, Eli," said Ben, swallowing his last bit of sausage.

"You ate them quickly," chortled Abel. "In fact you *wolfed* them down!" He grinned at his friends. "Did you get my pun? Their team is the *Wolves* and they *wolfed* down their sausages."

The gargoylz rolled around the tent chuckling, until a shrill blast from Miss Bleet's whistle made them freeze.

"Come on, Wolves and Bears!" they heard her yell. "At the double."

Max and Ben threw their clothes on and ran out to join the rest of the campers. Miss Bleet stood in the middle of the clearing. She had water bottles strapped to her belt, a pair of ancient binoculars round her neck and an enormous hat with corks hanging from it rammed on her head.

"Your first challenge today is a treasure hunt."

"Treasure hunt!" came an excited gargoyle squawk from the bushes behind Max and Ben. "I told you there'd be treasure, me hearties!"

Miss Bleet looked round sharply. "Who said that?" she demanded.

"Sorry, miss," said Ben quickly. "It was me. I got a bit over-excited. I love treasure hunts."

Miss Bleet peered at him severely through her corks. "You can only join in if you stop putting on silly voices."

She handed each team a map. "Wolves – you have to find three blue flags on your route, and Bears – you have to find three red flags. The first team to bring all their flags back will get a point – and some treasure. I've sent Mr Price and Mr Black into the woods to set out the flags."

Barry stuffed the map in his pocket. He unwrapped a piece of bubble gum,

shoved it in his mouth
and threw the silver
wrapper on the
ground. "Follow me,
you lot," he ordered.
"This is going
to be easy." He
looked over Lucinda's
shoulder at the Wolves'

map. "You'll never find your
flags," he sneered. "The treasure is ours."

"We were wrong about The Basher,
Agent Neal," Max whispered to Ben. "He's
being just as nasty as usual."

"You're right, Agent Black," Ben
whispered back. "He's forgotten about
being scared. We might need Secret Plan
Stage Two – Scare The Basher Even
More."

"Come on, Wolves," shouted Lucinda in
a commanding tone. "This way!"

"We're right behind you, Lucinda," said

Poppy and Tiffany together.

Duncan and Gavin followed the girls and Max and Ben trailed along at the back of the group.

"Bossy pants," muttered Ben. "This treasure hunt's going to be awful with *her* in charge."

"I expect the gargoylz have gone off on their own adventure," said Max miserably. "I wouldn't blame them."

At that moment, a huge oak tree overhead reached out a branch and hooked it round Lucinda's rucksack. She fell over backwards, waving her arms and legs and shrieking at the top of her voice.

The boys cheered up immediately.

"Cool trick, Abel!" whispered Max, patting his gnarly trunk. "She looks like an upside-down tortoise."

"You're the best tree in the whole forest," said Ben admiringly.

Poppy and Tiffany hoicked Lucinda to her feet and the Wolves set off again.

Abel scampered secretly ahead and turned into all sorts of trees that always seemed to catch at the girls' hair and ribbons, making them screech.

"Looks like this hunt's going to be fun after all," said Max as the boys heard muffled chortling sounds from the undergrowth.

At last Lucinda called a halt in a small

clearing. "Our first flag should be here!" she announced.

The Wolves hunted around.

"Are you sure we're in the right place?" asked Max after a while.

"Have you got the map upside down?" asked Ben.

"How rude!" said Tiffany.

"We're definitely in the right place," insisted Poppy. "It's the flag that isn't."

"It must be here somewhere," said Duncan.

"Let's search again," suggested Gavin.

Ben kneeled down and picked something up.

He beckoned to Max to follow him into the bushes and showed him what he'd found. It was a silver bubble-gum wrapper.

"Something very strange is going on here, Agent Black," said Ben. "This is exactly the type of gum The Basher was eating. And this wrapper still smells of mint, so it's only just been dropped."

"Well spotted, Agent Neal," agreed Max. "I bet he sneaked off from his trail, cut across and pinched our flag so we can't win. He is such a cheat!"

"Ahoy there, shipmatez!" came a squawk above their heads. Ira was peeping out from between some pine cones. "I've been

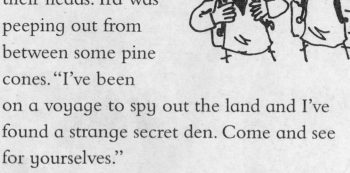

on a voyage to spy out the land and I've found a strange secret den. Come and see for yourselves."

The Wolves were still searching the clearing.

"Lead the way," said Max eagerly. "They're too busy to notice we've gone."

They sneaked off through the bushes. Ira suddenly stopped and flung out a wing.

"Here it be!" He pointed at a twisted, blackened tree. Its tangled mass of branches grew right down to the ground, and moss and

dead leaves covered it like a roof.

"Awesome!" breathed Max. "It's so dark and creepy."

"I can see eyes," whispered Ben in alarm. "There's something in there!"

With a roar, four stony little creatures burst out from the lair and knocked them flying.

"Tricked you!" yelled Eli, his snakes wriggling and giggling merrily.

"That was a cool prank," said Max. "We thought you were monsters!"

"Dangling drainpipes!" chuckled Toby. "I haven't enjoyed myself so much since Abel tapped his twigs on the vicar's door and every time he opened it there was no one there!"

Ben's eyes lit up. "I've had an awesome idea for Secret Plan Stage Two — Scare The Basher Even More. Remember the monster we told Barry about?"

"The monster with hundreds of sharp teeth and claws like knives?" said Max, an excited gleam in his eyes. "The one who eats kids for breakfast?"

"That's the one," said Ben eagerly. "What if Barry comes to this creepy den and actually *finds* the monster?"

"Brilliant plan," exclaimed Max. He

looked around at the eager
stony faces and gave Ben
a wink. "But where will
we find a scary monster?"

The gargoylz jumped
up and down in excitement.
"We'll do it!" they chanted.

"Why didn't we think of that?" said Ben
with a grin.

Azzan puffed a blast of smoke from his
nostrils. "We'll make sure it's got a scary
blast of fire . . ."

"And it'll be ever so growly," said Toby.

"And have loadz of sharp teeth,"
added Eli.

"And terrible clawz," said Abel.

"It'll be a fearsome sea monster," said
Ira. "Even though we be far from the
ocean."

"Cool!" said Max. "And tonight will
be the perfect time for Barry to meet our
monster."

"We'd better get back to our team," said Ben.

"I'll see if I can spot them," said Toby, whizzing up into the air.

He led them quickly back to where the Wolves were standing by a small rock. Lucinda, Poppy and Tiffany were snivelling, and Duncan and Gavin were studying the map and scratching their heads.

"Sorry," called Max as they joined the team. "We went the wrong way. Have we missed anything?"

"We can't find *any* flags!" wailed Poppy, wringing her hands.

"We followed the trail exactly," said Duncan. "The third flag should be right here, next to this tree stump."

"We must have been doing it wrong," sniffed Tiffany. "We didn't find the second flag either."

"The Wolves are going to lose!" cried Lucinda, pulling at her ponytail in despair.

"Let's go back," said Poppy miserably.

The girls trailed off down the path. The rest of the Wolves followed.

"We can't tell Miss Bleet about The Basher cheating," Ben whispered to Max. "We can't prove anything, even with the wrapper."

"And Barry will just beat us up!" replied Max. "But at least we'll get our own back with Secret Plan Stage Two."

As they reached the camp, they saw the Bears sitting by their campfire. They were eating chocolate coins.

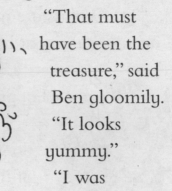

"That must have been the treasure," said Ben gloomily. "It looks yummy."

"I was wondering where you'd got to, Wolves," said Miss Bleet. "The Bears were back ages ago."

"We couldn't find our flags," said Max.

"You need more practice with your map reading," said their teacher. "Never mind. There'll be more challenges this afternoon for you to win some points." She marched off to whittle some sticks.

"Bears are the best!" shouted Barry.

He ran over and waved three bright
red flags in their faces. "We beat the
Wolves!" he chanted. "They're such wimps,
they couldn't even find their way on an
easy-peasy treasure hunt. They got lost

and they went boo-hoo-hoo all the way
home!" He dashed back to the Bears,
whacking his teammates' hands in a high
five and sending them flying. "I knew
they'd never find their flags . . . er, before
we found ours!"

"I can't *wait* for Secret Plan Stage Two," muttered Ben.

"We've got a problem, Agent Neal," said Max with a frown. "The Basher is such a scaredy-cat I bet he won't dare come out after dark."

"Good point, Agent Black," said Ben, scratching his head. Then an idea pinged into his brain. "I've got the answer. We'll tell Barry there's going to be scrummy food in the forest tonight. He's so greedy he won't be able to resist."

"Brilliant idea!" exclaimed Max. He marked the den on their map with an X. They strolled past Barry, who was still waving his flags and grinning evilly.

"That was an awesome den we found today in the woods," said Ben loudly.

"You mean the one that we marked with a big X on this map?" asked Max, flapping it so that The Basher couldn't miss it.

"That's the one," answered Ben. "I reckon we should go back there when everyone else is asleep."

Barry had stopped shouting. He stared at the boys, his eyes growing wider and wider.

"And we'll take scrummy food and have a secret feast!" Max said.

"I've brought some of my nan's cupcakes."

He let the map fall to the ground by Barry's feet, pretending he hadn't noticed.

"Good one!" whispered Ben as they walked away, stifling their giggles. "His ears are flapping."

Max sneaked a glance over his shoulder. "The plan's working. He's picked up the map."

"This is going to be awesome." Ben grinned. "The Basher has no idea what the gargoylz have got in store for him!"

4. The Monster of Ferny Forest

It was dark outside and the campsite was quiet. Max and Ben stuffed their clothes and rucksacks into their sleeping bags. The gargoylz were waiting in the bushes to set off on their mission.

"This is great superspy work, Agent Neal," said Max as they laid the lumpy bags down. "It really looks as if we're asleep in there."

"It's perfect, Agent Black," agreed Ben. "We'd win the 'Trick the grown-ups that we're still here' challenge easy-peasy."

"Shame we can't suggest it to Miss Bleet," said Max, grabbing his torch. "That would put the Wolves in the lead."

"We would have been in the lead anyway, if Barry hadn't cheated in the treasure hunt!" groaned Ben.

It had been a busy afternoon. Miss Bleet had set them two more challenges and now the score was two-all.

"We won the 'Make a stretcher out of woodland materials' challenge fair and square," said Max. "It wasn't our fault that the Bears' stretcher broke. Barry shouldn't have made them carry him on it."

"And we'd have won the 'Don't speak through dinnertime' challenge if Tiffany hadn't squealed," added Ben. "That spider that landed on her head was teeny weeny!" He listened hard. "I think everyone's gone to sleep," he hissed. "I can hear my dad snoring. Time for Secret Plan Stage Two – Scare The Basher Even More."

"We're going to need our best superspy creeping," whispered Max. He poked his head cautiously through the tent flap and crept out into the dark. Ben picked up his torch and followed.

A fearsome figure in white suddenly appeared in front of them. Max and Ben leaped in the air!

"What are you doing out here?" the figure demanded.

Then they realized the apparition was wearing a frilly white nightie.

"Lucinda!" gasped Ben. "We were just—"

"Get back to your tent right now!"
hissed Lucinda, her ponytail whipping
furiously from side to side. "If Miss Bleet
finds you creeping about we'll lose points
and then we won't get the prize and it
will be all your fault and—
Ahhhhh . . . !" Lucinda
dived headfirst
into her tent as
a small grass
snake slithered
past.

"You stay in
there, Lucinda,"
said Max. "It's a
night-time snake.
It won't be gone
till morning."

"Thanks, Eli!" Ben
whispered as the rest of the
gargoylz popped out of the bushes. "It's
safe to go, everyone."

The boys and gargoylz tiptoed out of the campsite.

"I'll be leader," said Toby. "Follow me!"

"I'm the captain so I say who's the leader!" squawked Ira. "Toby, you're the leader!"

Toby snatched up Ben's torch and flew in front of them, lighting the way.

"Everything looks different at night," said Max as they crept through the dark forest. "The trees are awesomely spooky!"

Ben jumped as something prodded him in the back.

"Awesomely spiky, you mean!" came a cheerful voice. Abel had turned into a tree and was waving his twiggy branches at them.

"We've arrived!" exclaimed Toby. The den loomed up ahead. It looked even more mysterious – and spooky – in the torchlight.

The gargoylz dashed inside and the light bobbed about, showing an excited tangle of stony ears and tails.

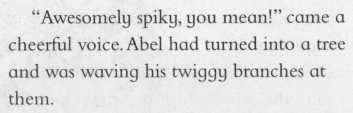

Then it went out. "Wait there, boyz," ordered Ira. "Me and

my shipmates are going to get The Basher's surprise ready."

Through the darkness Max and Ben could hear scuffles and snorts, and at last a curious shape burst out of the den. The torch clicked on and the boys jumped in fright at the sight before their eyes. A hideous spiky monster was towering over them. Its body was gnarled and knobbly, and it was

wrapped in a long flowing cloak. From the
top of the cloak two heads emerged – one
with a fierce beak and the other with an
evil, grinning monkey face. A hissing snake
curled round them both, its black spots
glowing eerily in the strange light coming
out of the cloak.

"That's . . . brilliant!" croaked Max
when he'd recovered from the shock.

"Awesome!" agreed Ben, trying to stop
his knees knocking.

"Glad you like it!" squawked Ira. "We
borrowed one of the spare
tentz for the cloak."

"And I'm
holding
the torch
under
our
chinz
to
make

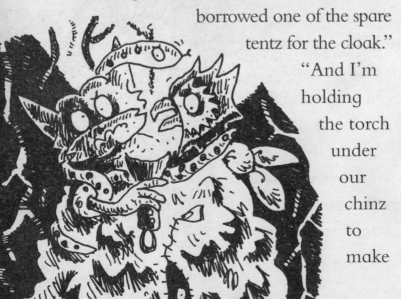

us really creepy," chuckled Toby, waving it at the boys.

"It's the scariest monster in the history of scary monsters!" Max told them. "But where's Azzan?"

A huge burst of flame belched from the creature's belly. "Here I am!" The dragony gargoyle popped his head out and gave the boys a wave.

"My fire will give The Basher the biggest fright of all," he declared.

"No it won't," said Toby.

"My evil glowing face will scare him the most."

"My hisssing will make him ssscarper," said Eli.

"I'm the captain," began Ira. "So I'll say who—"

"Shh!" cried Ben suddenly. "I can hear something."

Heavy footsteps were stomping towards them.

"Max Black and Ben Neal," came Barry's voice. "You can't keep secrets from me. Give me your food!"

"It's The Basher!" whispered Max urgently. "Are you ready, monster?"

"Ready!" came a deep chorus of growls.

"Then get back in your den and turn off the torch until he comes into view," Ben told them. "And no more arguing!"

Max and Ben tucked themselves behind a bush. The Basher's footsteps were coming closer. "Very clever sneaking out for a feast and not telling anyone – I don't think. Well, it's not fair. I'm going to have all the goodies, not you!"

"He's trying to be big and brave," whispered Max. "But he sounds scared."

The footsteps stopped at the den. "I know you're in there," Barry shouted, rattling the branches. "It's no use trying to hide— What was that?"

The next second he let out an ear-splitting screech that Lucinda would have been proud of. "A monster . . . It's the monster of Ferny Forest!"

The boys looked through the leaves. The gargoyle monster was lumbering out of its den, the eyes on its two faces glaring fiercely in the torchlight. The monster's twiggy hands waved menacingly in the air and flames shot out from its belly with a loud *whoosh!*

"*Hisss!*" went the writhing snake.

"Heh! Heh! Heh!" cackled the monkey head.

"Shiver me timberz!" squawked the other head. "I mean . . . *grrr!* I'm a fierce monster and I'm coming after you, Barry Price."

For a moment Barry stood rooted to the spot, shaking like a jelly. The boys rammed their fists in their mouths to stifle their giggles. Then Barry was off,

crashing away through the bushes.

"It's going to get me!" His shrieking echoed around the trees. "I want my dad! Help!"

The monster tottered after him for a few steps, then collapsed in a heap. The gargoylz scrambled out, rolling about with laughter.

"Were we good?" asked Azzan eagerly. "You were fantastic!" said Ben. "Secret Plan Stage Two worked brilliantly."

"Now we'll take a shortcut back," said Max, "before The Basher gets there and wakes everyone up. We don't want to be seen sneaking in."

"We'll get in our tent and pretend we've been there all along," agreed Ben.

They raced through the trees, dived into their tent and came out wearing their best sleepy expressions.

"Campsite chaos!" laughed Ben.

Barry Price was racing around the
tents, tripping over guy ropes and crashing
into pots and pans in his panic. "There's
a monster," he yelled, "and it's
after me!"

Tents zipped open and
sleepy campers emerged, rubbing their
eyes. They gathered around Barry, who
was flapping his arms about wildly.

Miss Bleet appeared in baggy pyjamas
and hair curlers. "What is going on,

Barry?" she demanded.

"There was a monster in the forest . . ." gulped The Basher, looking round wildly as if he expected it to appear any moment.

"There were never monsters in the forest when I was a Cub," said Max's dad.

"If my boy says there's a monster, there's a monster," declared Big Basher.

"Stop this at once!" ordered Miss Bleet. "You've had a nightmare, Barry, that's all. Get back to your tent." She glared at Mr Price. "There are no monsters in Ferny Forest."

"I'm not sleeping in a tent ever again!" wailed Barry.

Big Basher marched up to his son, hands on his hips. "I'm ashamed of you, boy," he growled in his ear. "Making all

this fuss over a silly dream. Now pipe
down and let us all get some sleep."

"I won't pipe down until Miss lets me
sleep in the motor home," insisted Barry.
"I'll keep everyone awake – all night!"

Miss Bleet huffed and produced the key
from her pyjama pocket.

Barry snatched it from her hand,
picked up his sleeping bag
and ran into the motor
home, slamming the
door in his dad's
face.

Miss Bleet
waved the campers
back to their
beds. "Quickly
now, back to your
tents, everyone," she
ordered. "And I don't
want to hear a peep out of anyone until
the morning!"

The gargoylz had already made themselves comfortable in the boys' sleeping bags when they got back to their tent. Max and Ben edged into the two tiny narrow spaces left.

"We're not in the way, are we?" Toby asked Ben. "Only it's so snug here."

"No problem," said Ben, "as long as you keep your tail out of my ear."

"You all deserve a nice place to sleep, after your awesome performance in the woods," said Max.

"Did you see The Basher's face when Toby turned on the torch?" said Abel, waving his twiggy arms and poking Max in the nose.

"I nearly deafened him with my fan-tassstic hisssing," said Eli.

"I haven't laughed so much since Eli slithered into the vicar's bed and he thought his duvet was haunted," chuckled Toby.

"If The Basher thinks there's a monster on the loose, he won't be so nasty tomorrow and we'll all be able to have some fun," yawned Ben.

Max sighed. "It's a shame about the treasure hunt though. It would have been nice to have won that chocolate," he added sleepily.

The next morning Max and Ben were woken by the sound of Miss Bleet's angry voice. They leaped out of their sleeping bags and went to see what was going on. The gargoylz sneaked into the bushes to watch.

Barry was standing on the steps of the motor home. He looked very sheepish. Miss Bleet was holding something in her hands.

"She's got the blue flags from the treasure hunt!" exclaimed Max. "The ones we were meant to find. How . . . ?"

"What's going on?" demanded Mr Price, stumbling out of his tent.

"I've just been into your motor home to check that Barry was all right and I found these poking out of his sleeping

bag," declared Miss Bleet, shaking the flags under Big Basher's nose. "It explains why the Wolves couldn't find any yesterday. Barry had taken them."

"It was a joke," wailed The Basher.

"We didn't have that sort of joke when I was in the Cubs," said Max's dad.

"If my boy says it was a joke, it was a joke," muttered Big Basher.

"It was cheating!" said Miss Bleet

severely. "Barry, you have made your team
lose a point." She turned to the campers,
who had crowded round to see what was
going on. "I declare the Wolves the winners
of the treasure hunt, and that makes them
the winners of the whole weekend, as they
now have three points to one."

She delved into her huge shorts pockets
and handed boxes to all the cheering
Wolves. Duncan and Gavin slapped each
other on the back and the girls skipped
about in delight. Max and Ben punched
the air.

"You can open them when you get back to your tents," she said. "But now we must get ready for today's activities. As soon as you're ready we're going to Monkey Fun."

"Monkey Fun!" exclaimed Max. "That climbing place with all those ropes and walkways?"

"And zip wires?" added Ben.

"That's the one," said Miss Bleet, beaming. "It's in the forest, not far from here. We'll be there in no time."

"If it's in the forest I'm not going," said Barry. "I've . . . er . . . twisted my ankle." He began to limp about. "Wouldn't be safe. My dad can take me home instead."

"Nonsense," said Miss Bleet. "No one goes home early on my camping weekends! You can walk round with me."

Barry began to gibber.

"He thinks the monster will get him," Max whispered to Ben. "But I'm glad he's too scared to climb at Monkey Fun. He'd probably have pushed us all off the trees."

"Everyone get dressed," ordered Miss Bleet. "Then we can go. We'll have a special breakfast when we get there."

Max's dad rubbed his hands together. "We never had anything like that when I was in the Cubs," he said happily.

Max and Ben raced back to their tent, where their five grinning gargoyle friends were waiting for them.

"Put it there, gargoylz!" cried Ben, holding up his hand. "We couldn't have won the challenges without you!"

"And now we're off to Monkey Fun!" whooped Max as they all collapsed in a

high-five tangle. "And you can come too."

"Yippee!" shouted Azzan, jumping about on Ben's sleeping bag and scorching his pillow.

The boys flung down their boxes and pulled on their clothes.

"Aren't you going to open these?" asked Toby, giving Ben's prize a shake.

Max pulled on his T-shirt. "No time," he said. "We've got trees to climb and zip wires to zip down. Anyway, knowing Miss Bleet they're probably fluffy earmuffs . . ."

". . . or cuddly tortoises," added Ben as he quickly tied his shoelaces.

The gargoylz dived on the boxes, ripped off the plastic covers and opened the lids.

"They don't look fluffy to me," said Azzan.

"Or cuddly," said Abel.

"They've got strapsss," said Eli as all his snakes tried to look at once.

"To go on your wrists," squawked Ira.

"It's a digital watch!" cried Max, picking his up.

"With a compass!" exclaimed Ben. He strapped his on his wrist.

"And an alarm and a torch and loads of other functions!" said Max. "Great for our superspying!"

"My superspying skills tell me one thing, Agent Black," said Ben with a grin. "This has been a great weekend. We've beaten The Basher and now we're off to Monkey Fun!"

"And my superspying skills tell me that we've got the best friends in the history of best friends!" declared Max.

COLLECT ALL THE GARGOYLZ TITLES

Four stories packed full of magic, mischief and mayhem in every book!

There's more mischief, mayhem and magic at...

www.Gargoylz.co.uk

- Discover Gargoylz facts, sneaky stories and tricks plus info on all the books

- Send cheeky Gargoylz eCardz to all your friends!

- Sign up to receive a Secret Agent Gargoylz pack, with pesky pranks and lots of other fun things to do

log on to www.gargoylz.co.uk today!